W9-CBG-245

Autauga-Prattville
Public Library
254 Doster Street
Prattville, AL  36067

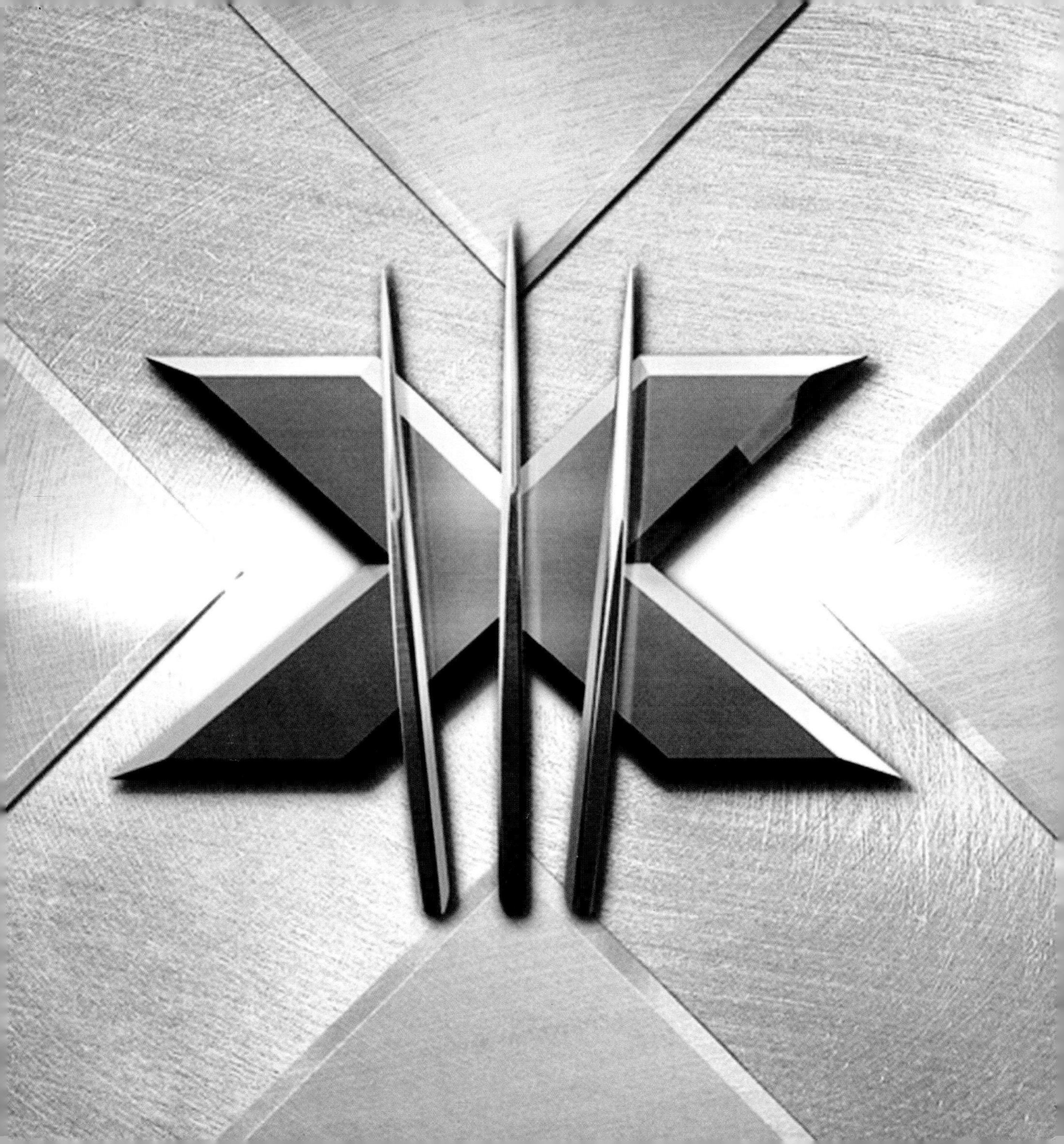

HarperCollins®, ☰®, and HarperKidsEntertainment™ are trademarks of HarperCollins Publishers.

X-Men: The Last Stand: Beast Chooses Sides
Marvel, X-Men and all related character names and the distinctive likenesses thereof are trademarks of Marvel Characters, Inc.
and are used with permission. Copyright © 2006 Marvel Characters, Inc. All rights reserved.
www.marvel.com
© 2006 Twentieth Century Fox Film Corporation
Printed in the United States of America.
No part of this book may be used or reproduced in any manner whatsoever without written permission
except in the case of brief quotations embodied in critical articles and reviews.
For information address HarperCollins Children's Books, a division of HarperCollins Publishers,
1350 Avenue of the Americas, New York, NY 10019.
www.harperchildrens.com
Book designed by John Sazaklis
Library of Congress catalog card number: 2006920161
ISBN-10: 0-06-082202-3—ISBN-13: 978-0-06-082202-6
2 3 4 5 6 7 8 9 10
❖
First Edition

$13.96   E MAP 11-20-07

# THE LAST STAND

Autauga-Prattville
Public Library
254 Doster Street
Prattville, AL   3606̅7̅

## BEAST CHOOSES SIDES

**Adapted By Catherine Hapka**

**Illustrations by Steven E. Gordon**

**Based on the motion picture screenplay**

**written by Simon Kinberg & Zak Penn**

**HarperKidsEntertainment**
*An Imprint of HarperCollinsPublishers*

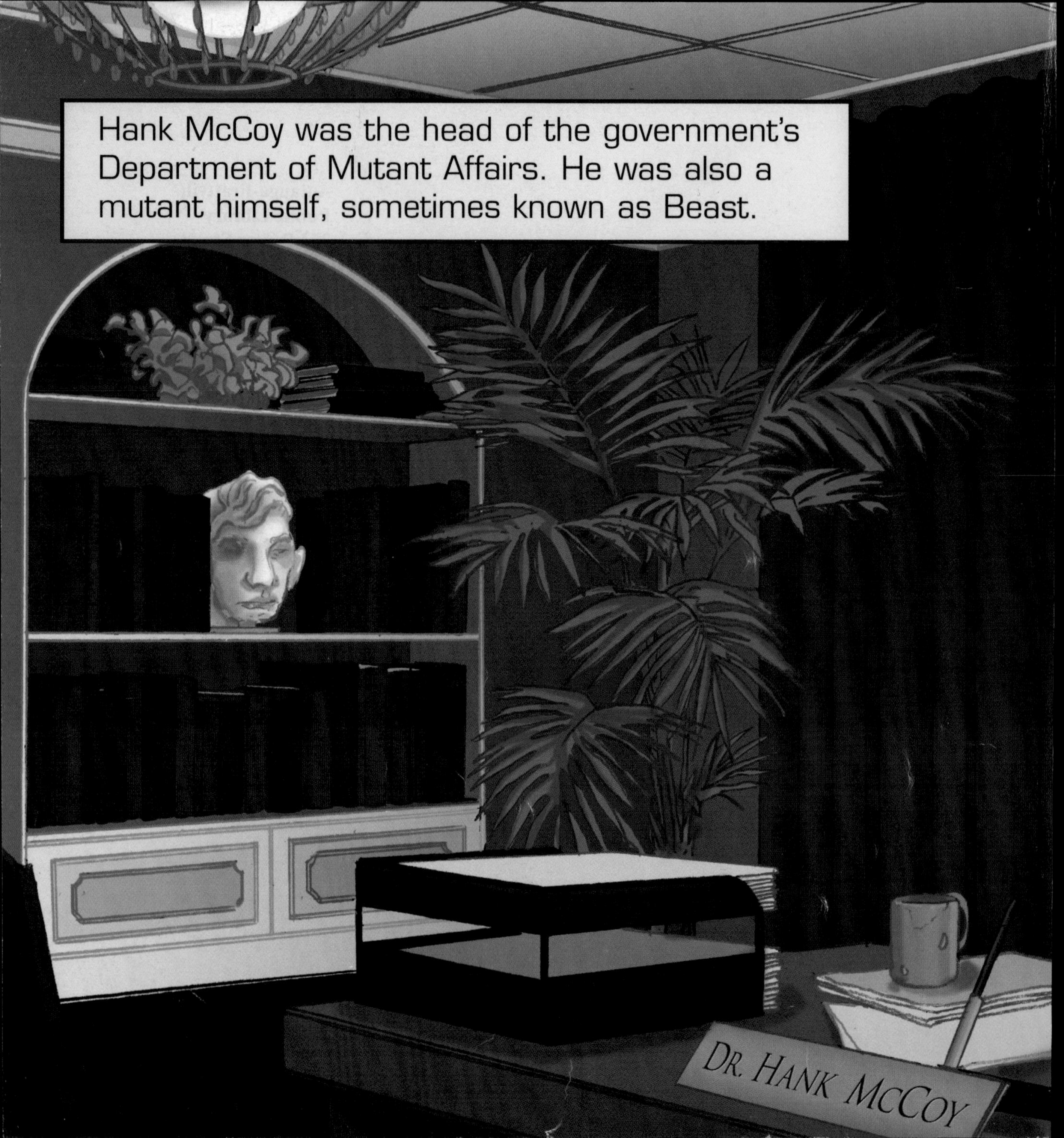
Hank McCoy was the head of the government's Department of Mutant Affairs. He was also a mutant himself, sometimes known as Beast.
DR. HANK McCOY

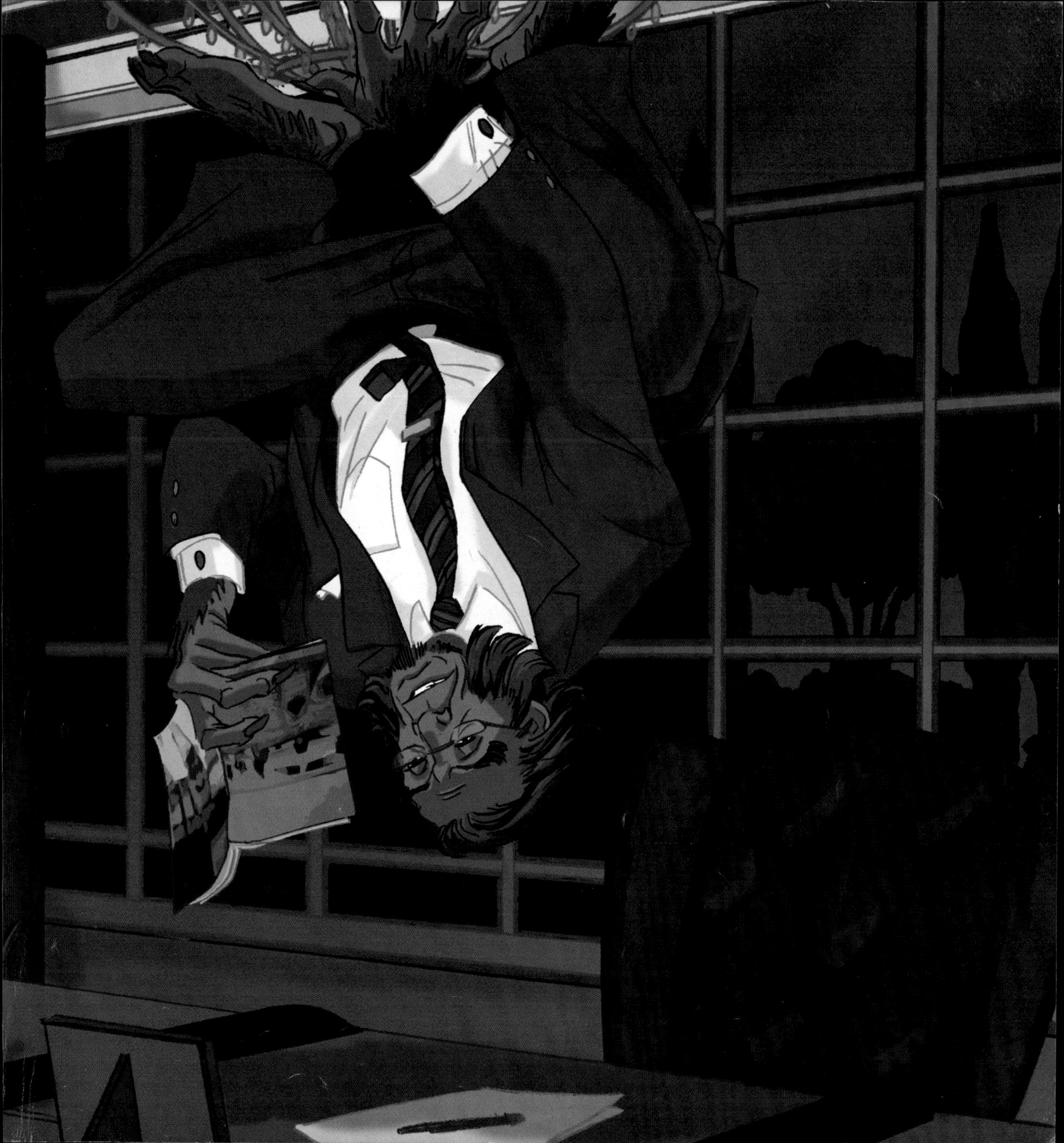

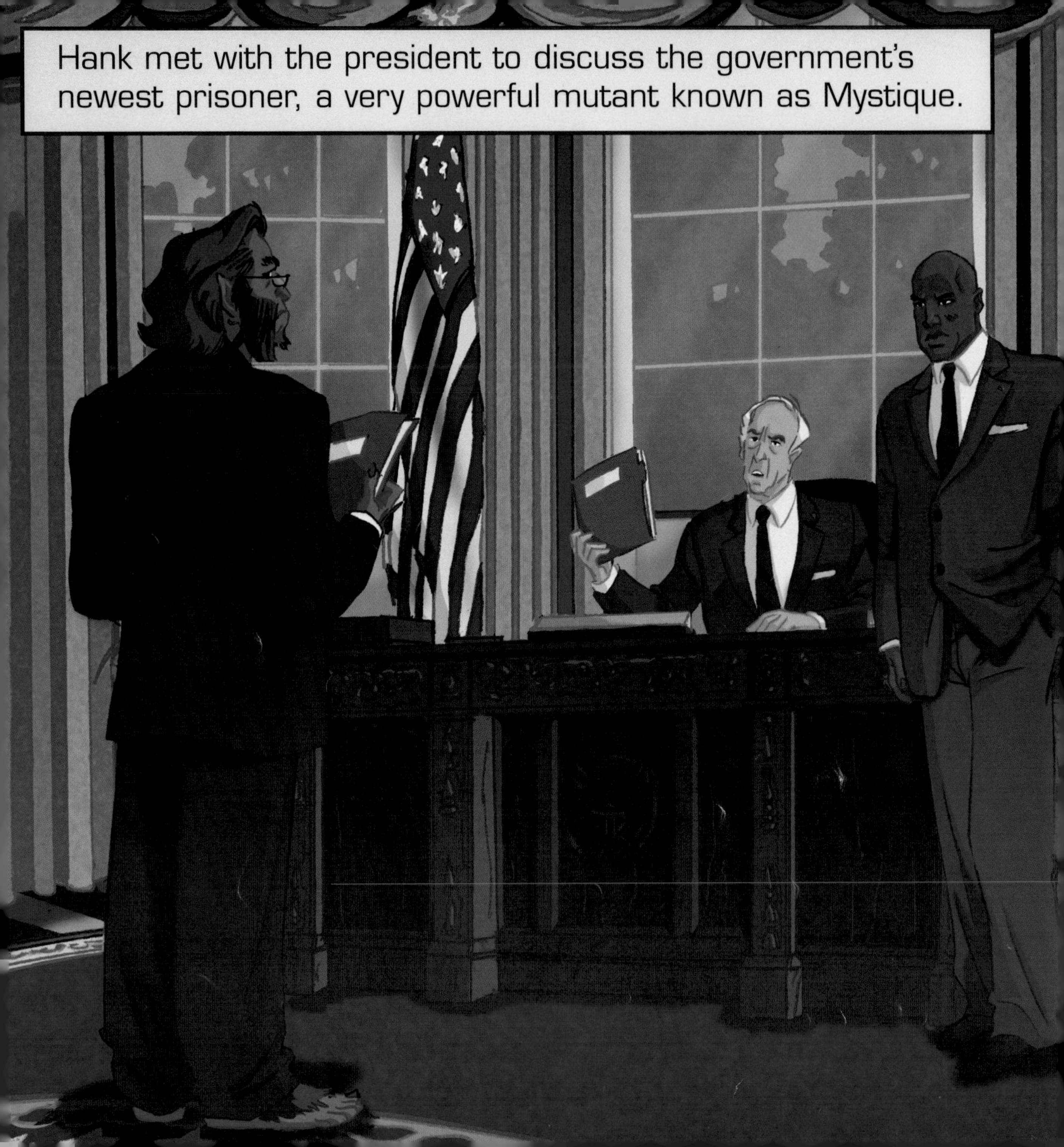
Hank met with the president to discuss the government's newest prisoner, a very powerful mutant known as Mystique.

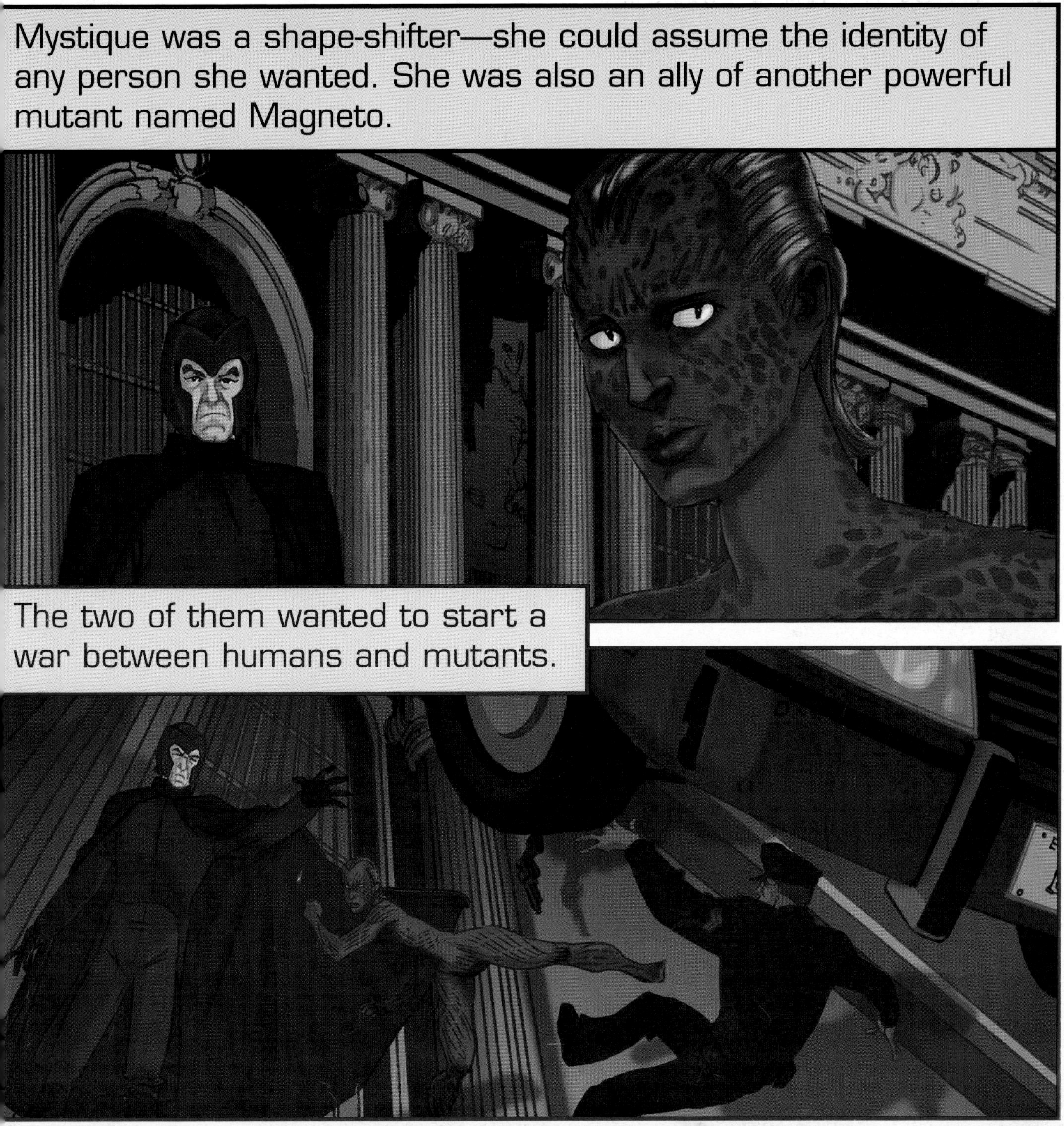
Mystique was a shape-shifter—she could assume the identity of any person she wanted. She was also an ally of another powerful mutant named Magneto.
The two of them wanted to start a war between humans and mutants.

YOU THINK YOUR WALLS CAN HOLD HER?
THEY FORM NEW POWERS, WE FORM NEW PRISONS. WE'LL BE A STEP AHEAD THIS TIME.

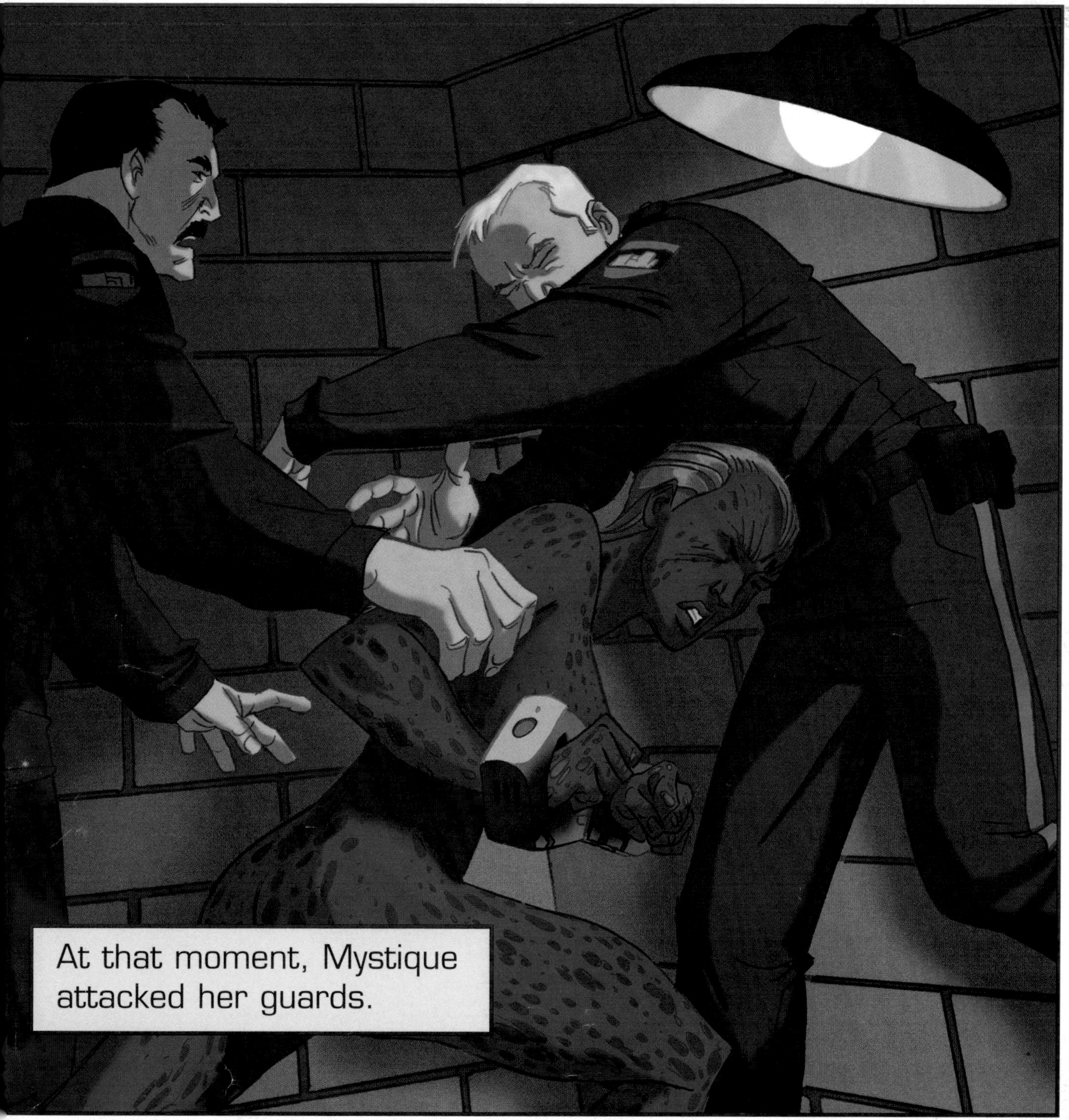
At that moment, Mystique attacked her guards.

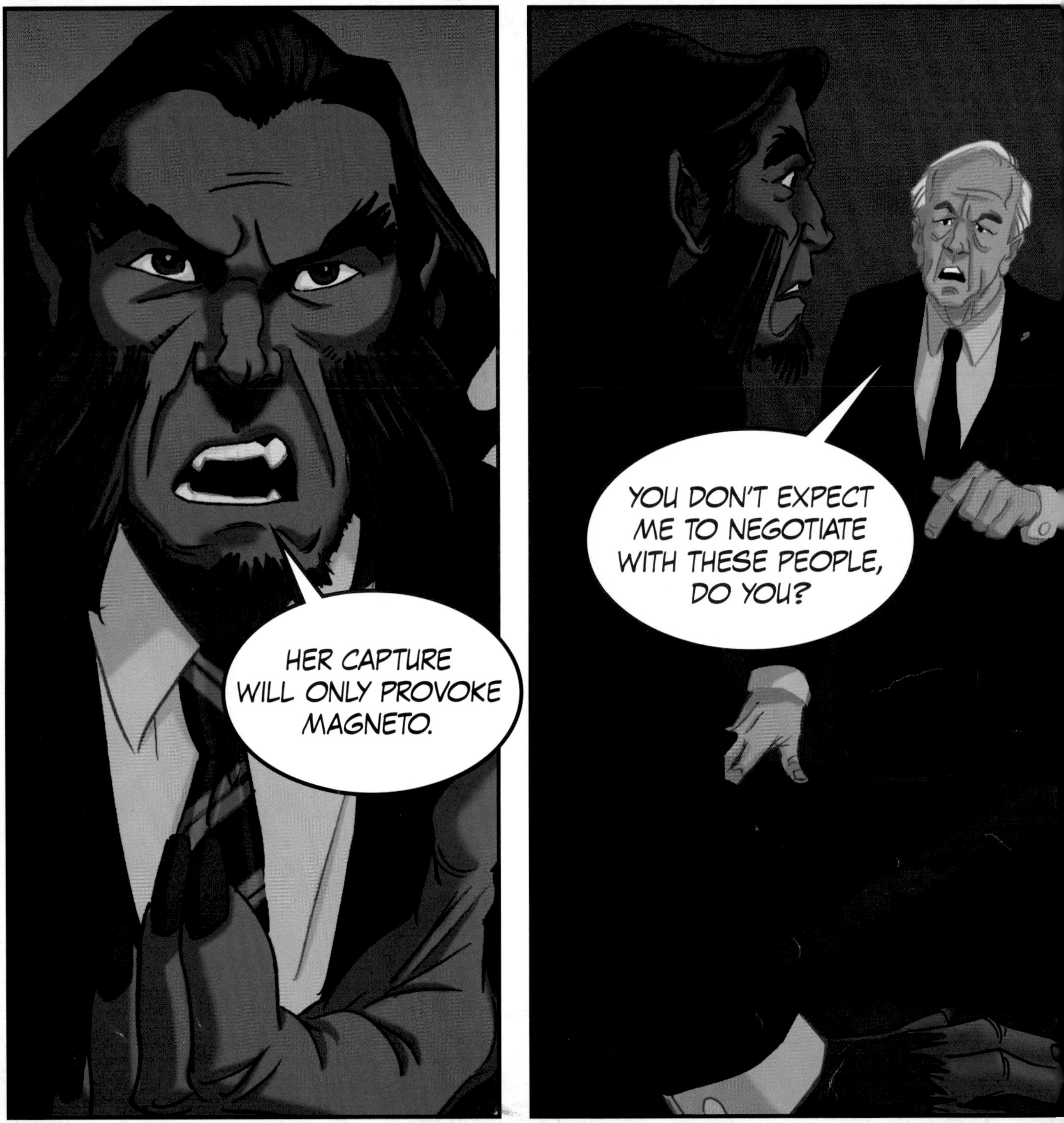
HER CAPTURE WILL ONLY PROVOKE MAGNETO.
YOU DON'T EXPECT ME TO NEGOTIATE WITH THESE PEOPLE, DO YOU?

Beast was surprised by the president's sharp answer.
I THOUGHT THAT WAS WHY YOU APPOINTED ME.

But the meeting wasn't just about Mystique's capture. The real reason the president had called them together was to talk about something else: a brand-new secret cure for the mutant gene.

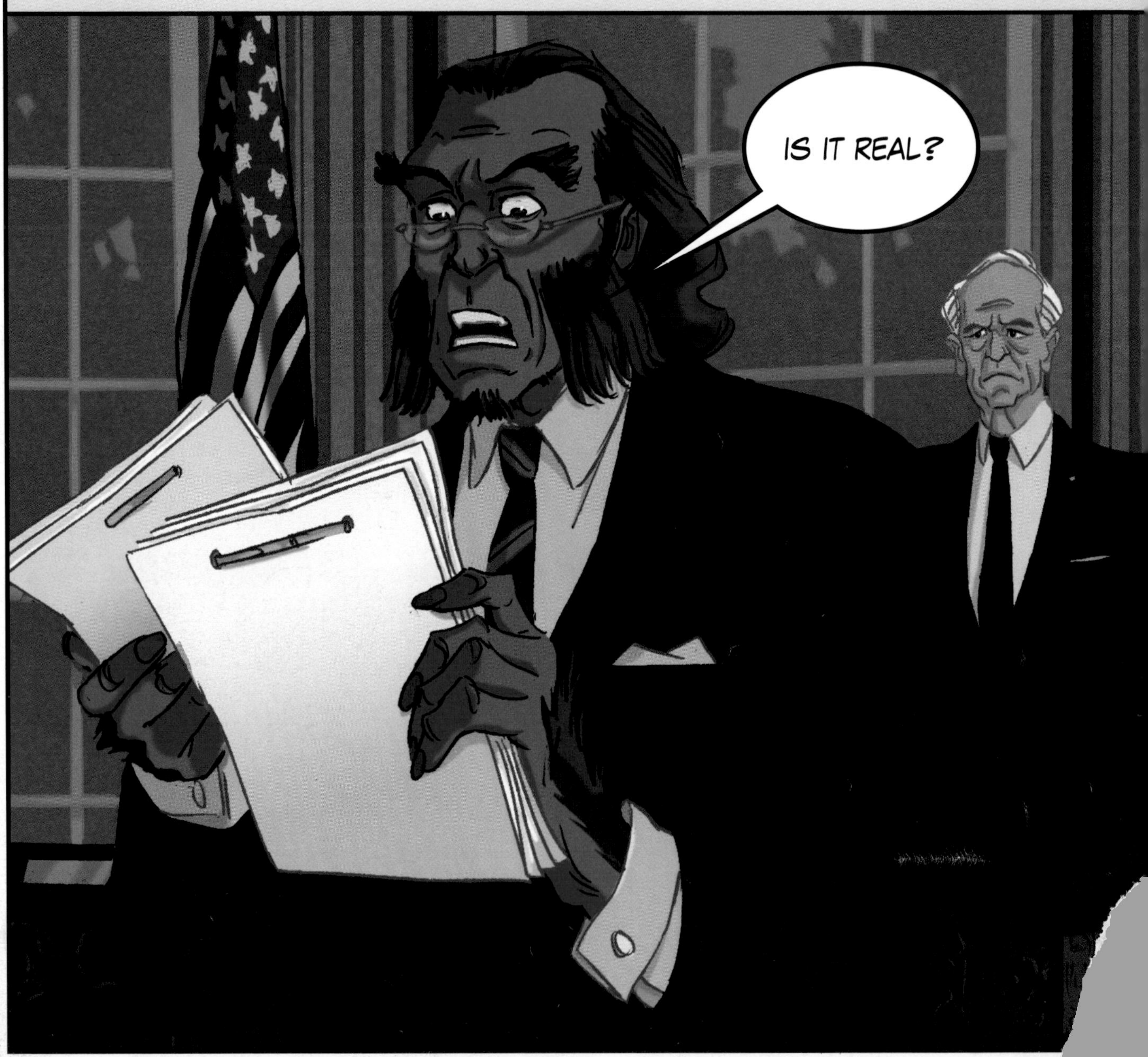
IS IT REAL?

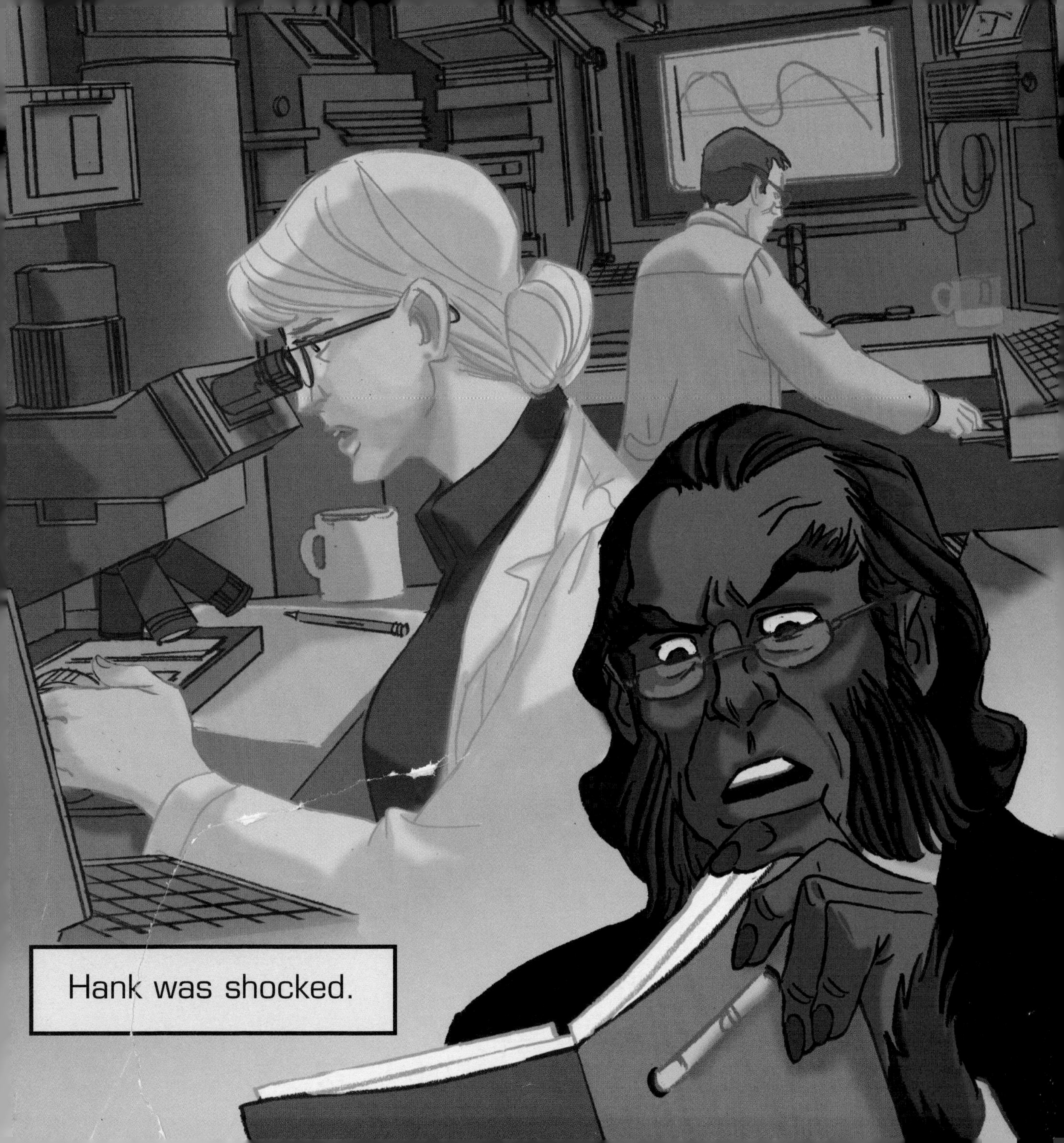
Hank was shocked.

Hank wasn't sure what to think about the new cure. He went to alert his friends, the X-Men, a group of mutants who ran a special school to help fellow mutants.

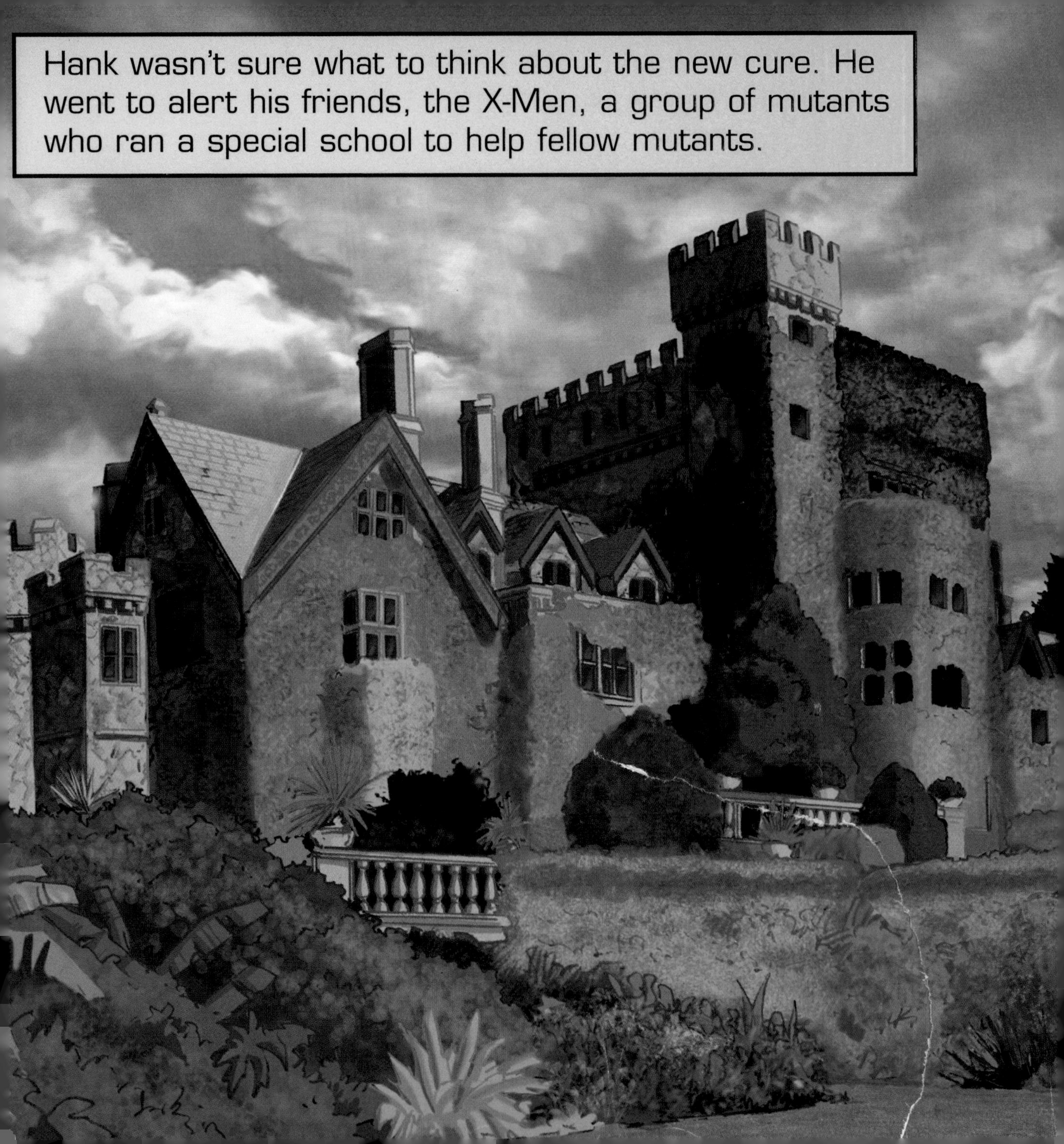

A COMPANY HAS DEVELOPED A MUTANT ANTIBODY. A WAY TO SUPPRESS THE MUTANT X GENE . . . PERMANENTLY.
SINCE WHEN IS IT A DISEASE? WHO WOULD WANT THIS CURE?

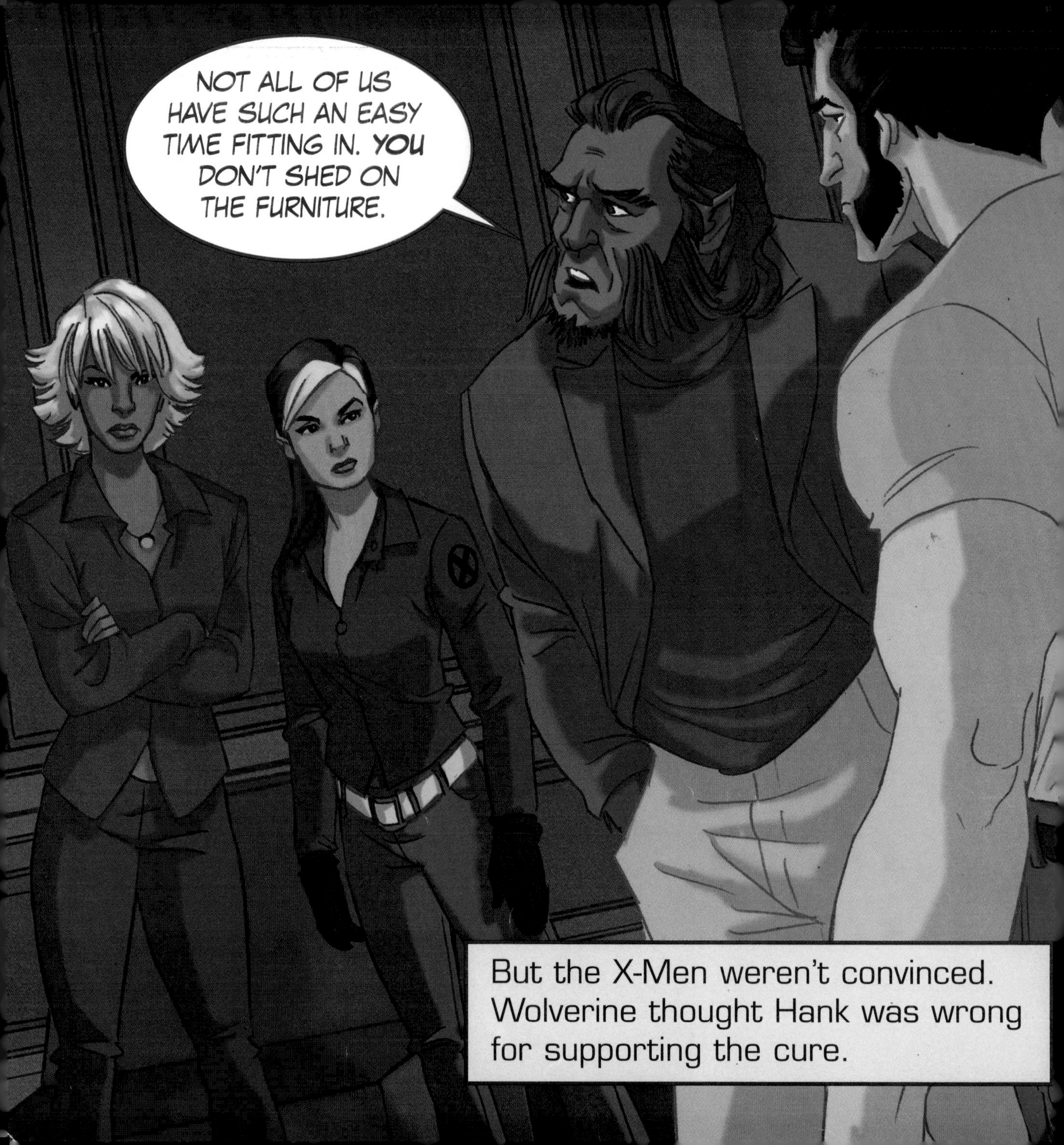
NOT ALL OF US HAVE SUCH AN EASY TIME FITTING IN. YOU DON'T SHED ON THE FURNITURE.
But the X-Men weren't convinced. Wolverine thought Hank was wrong for supporting the cure.

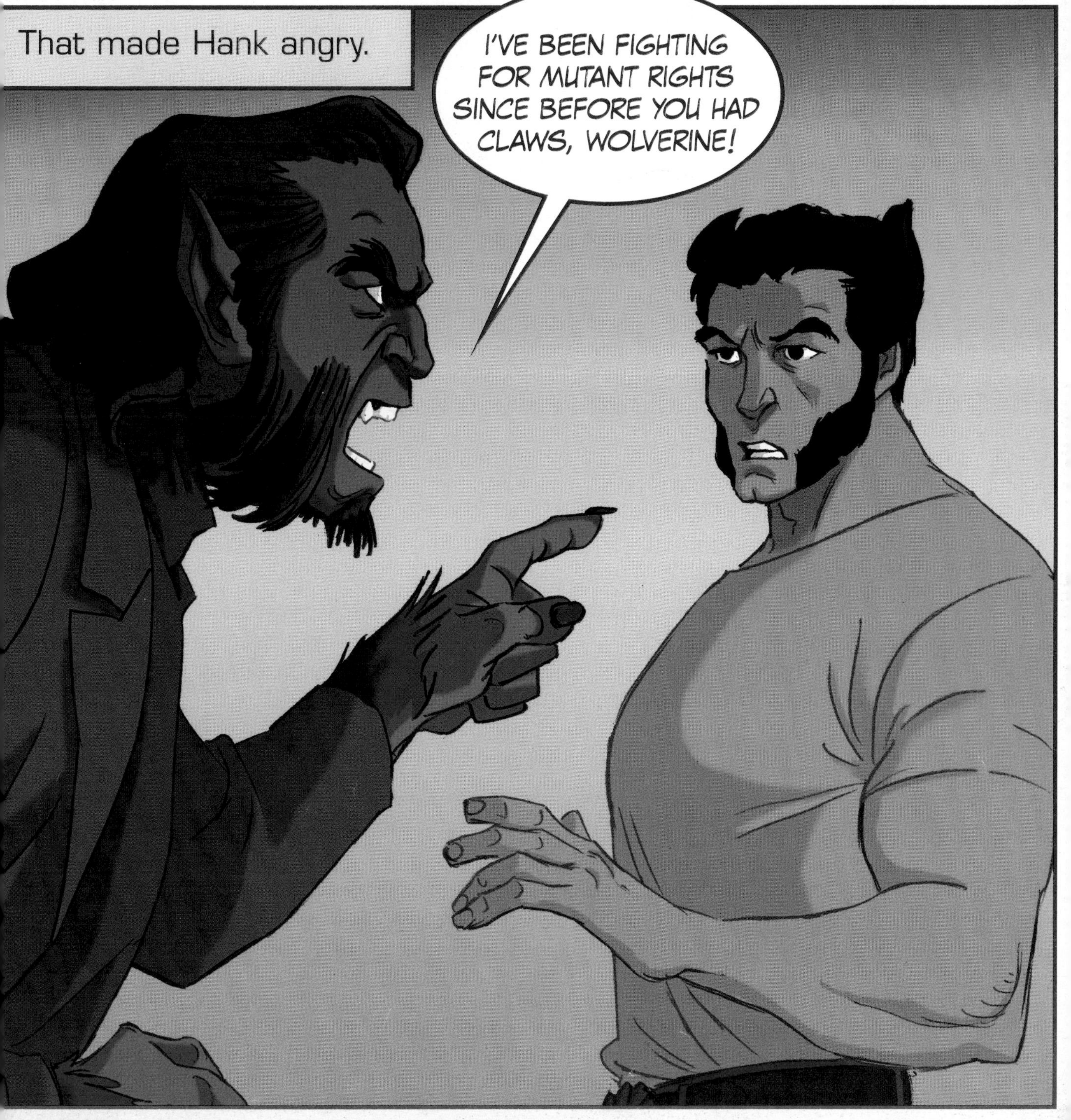
That made Hank angry.
I'VE BEEN FIGHTING FOR MUTANT RIGHTS SINCE BEFORE YOU HAD CLAWS, WOLVERINE!

All over the world, mutants were having the same discussions and arguments. Some wanted to be cured, while others didn't.

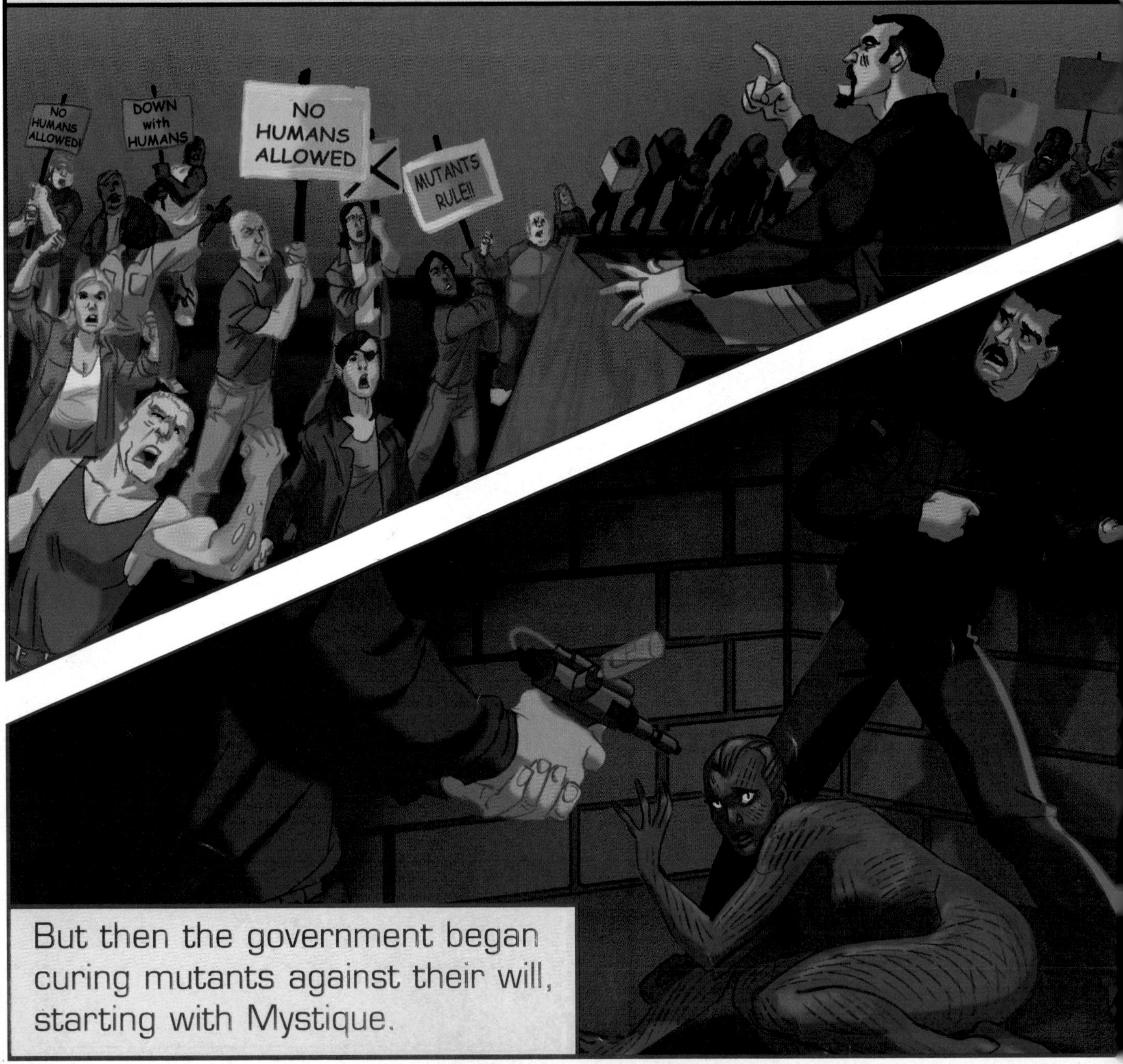
NO HUMANS ALLOWED!
DOWN with HUMANS
NO HUMANS ALLOWED
MUTANTS RULE!!
But then the government began curing mutants against their will, starting with Mystique.

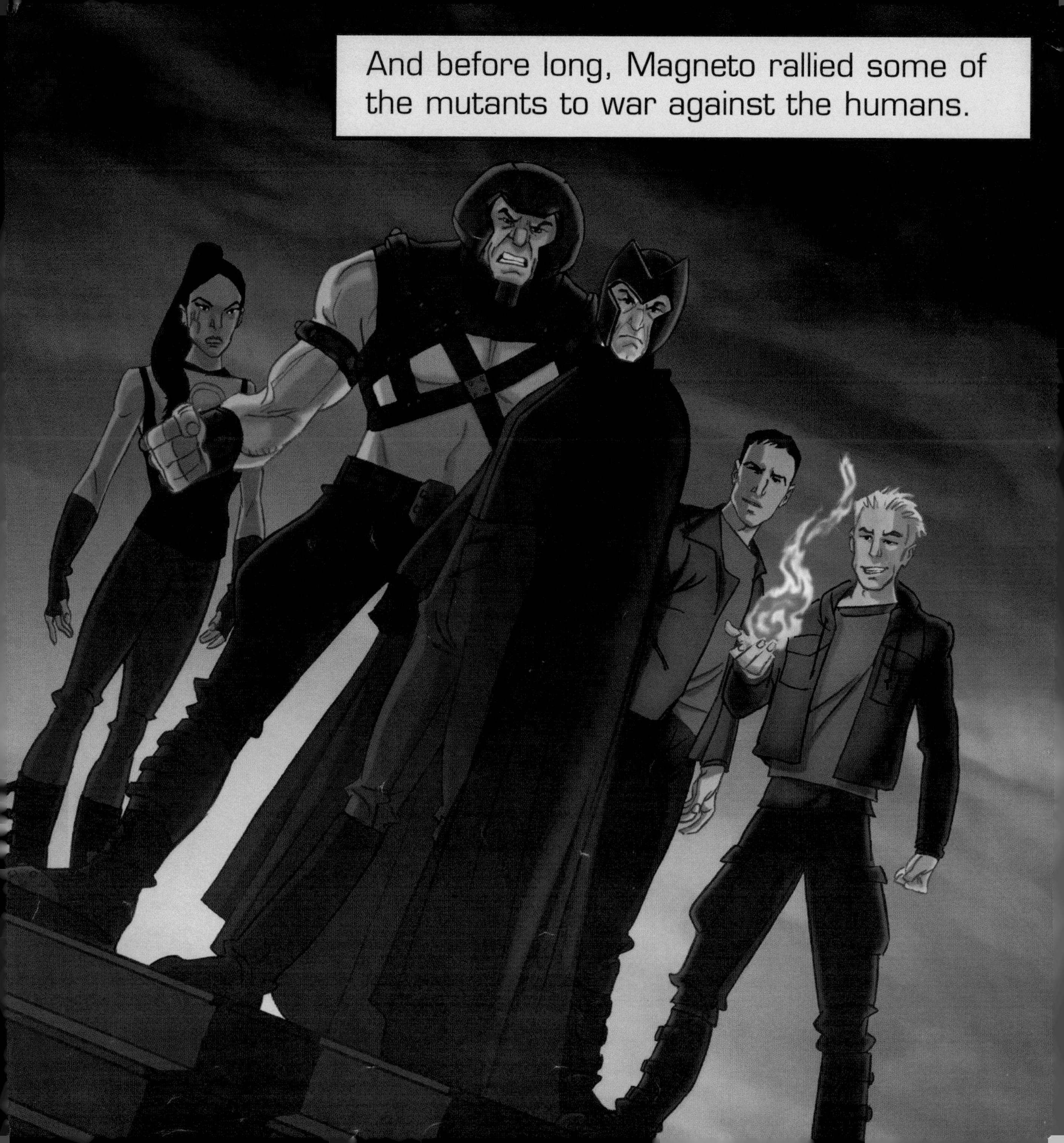
And before long, Magneto rallied some of the mutants to war against the humans.

That's when Hank knew exactly what to do. First he resigned from his government position.

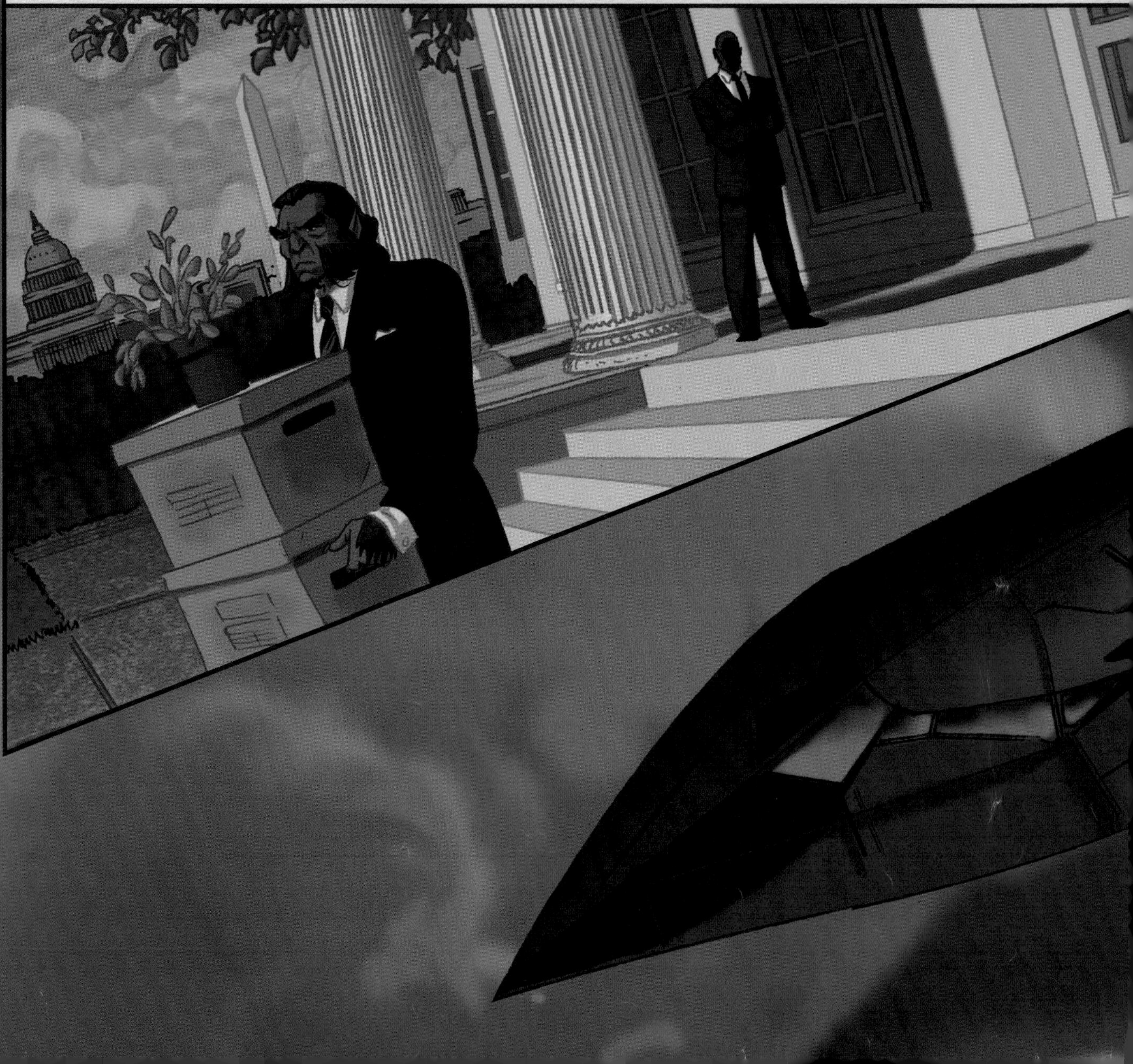

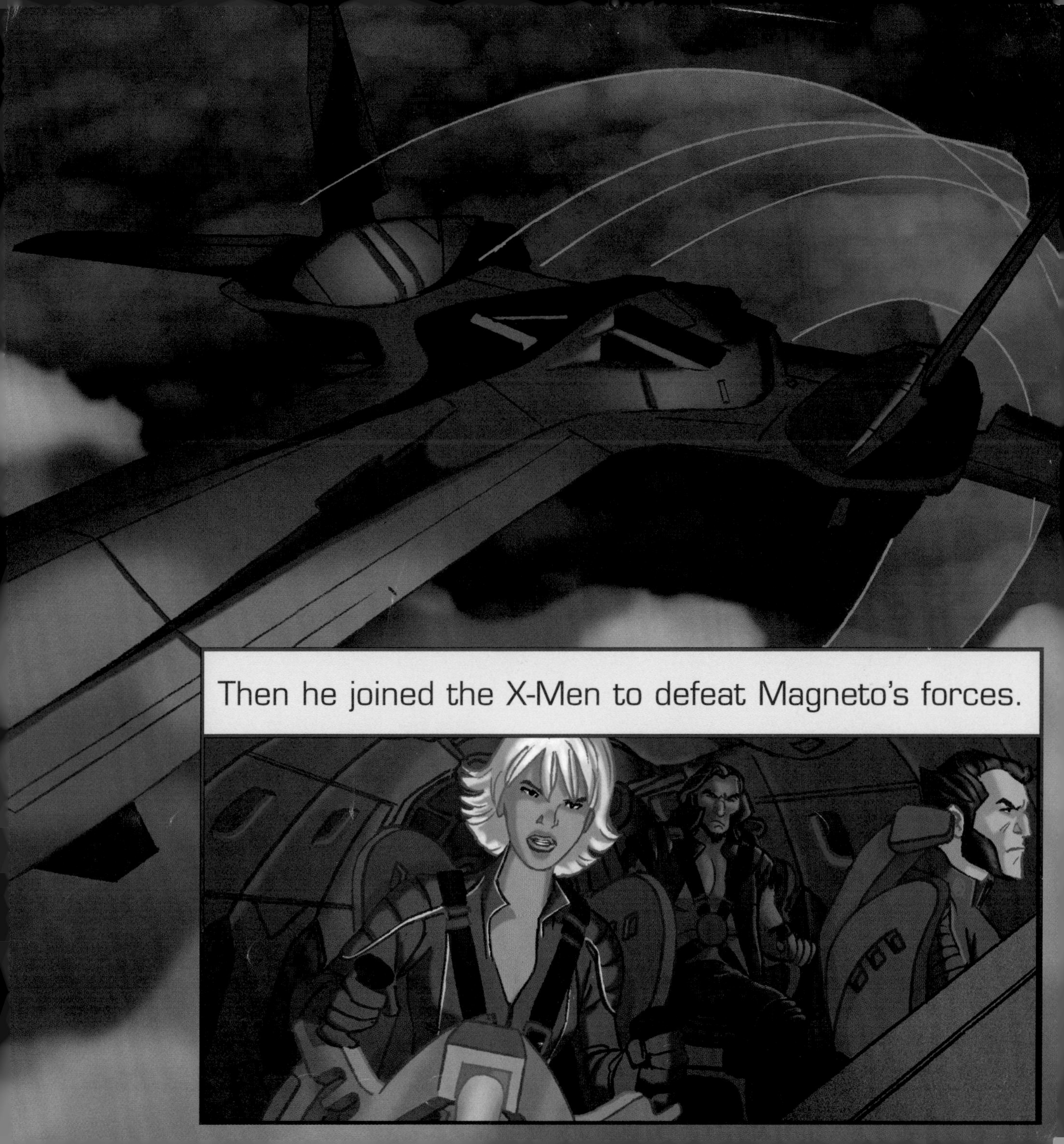
Then he joined the X-Men to defeat Magneto's forces.

The battle raged at the lab in California where the cure was made. Hank fought bravely alongside the other X-Men.

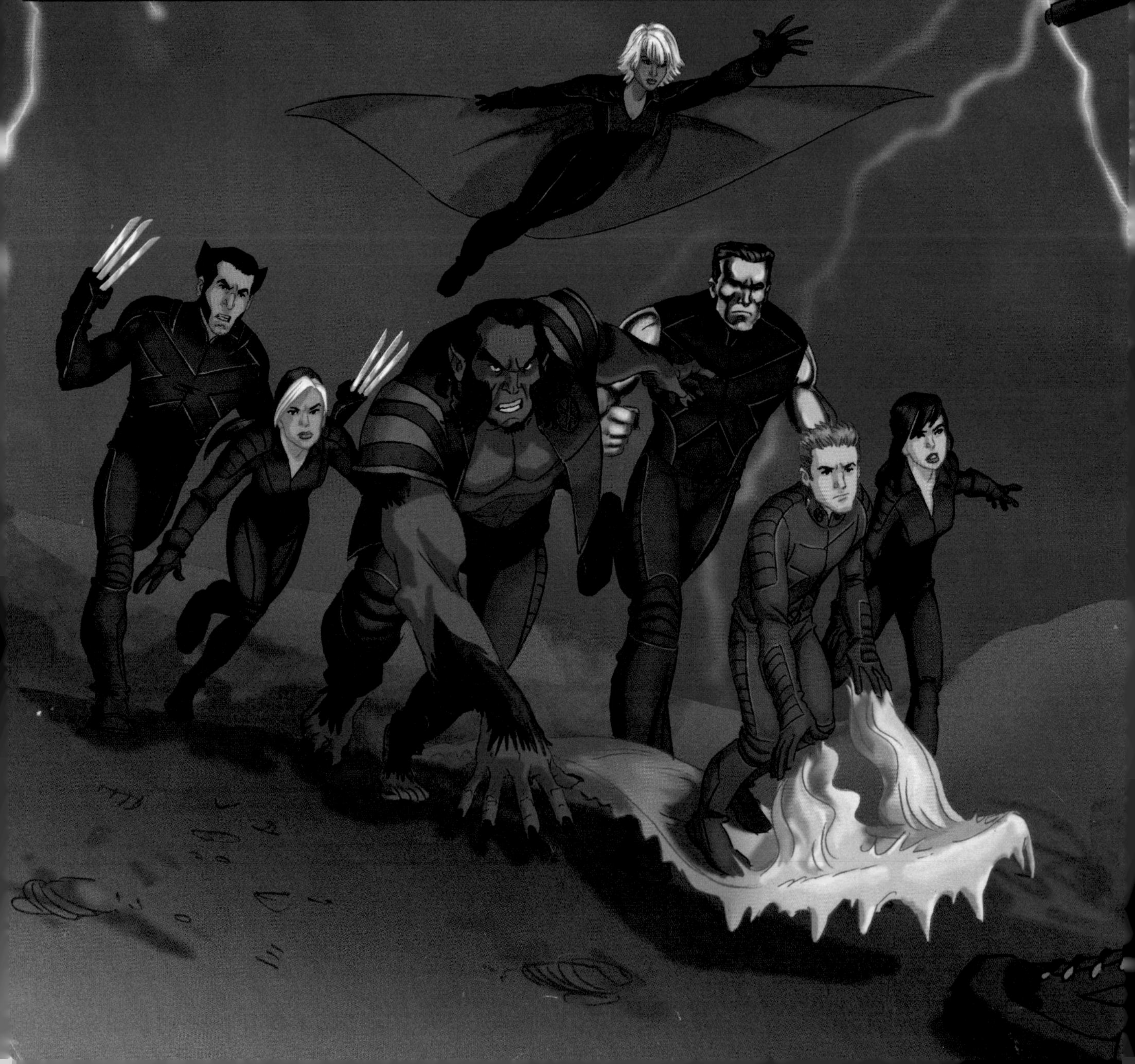

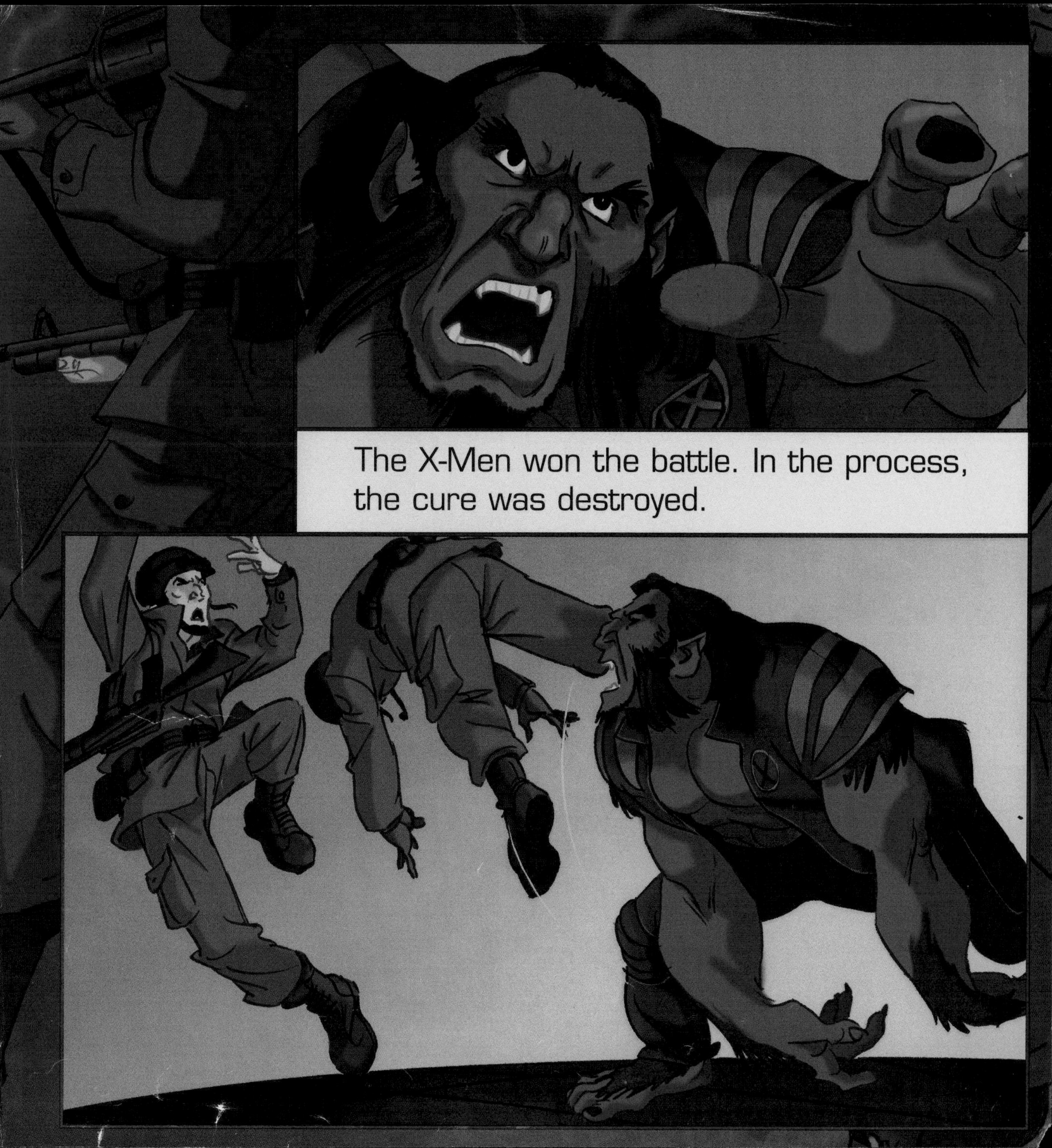
The X-Men won the battle. In the process, the cure was destroyed.

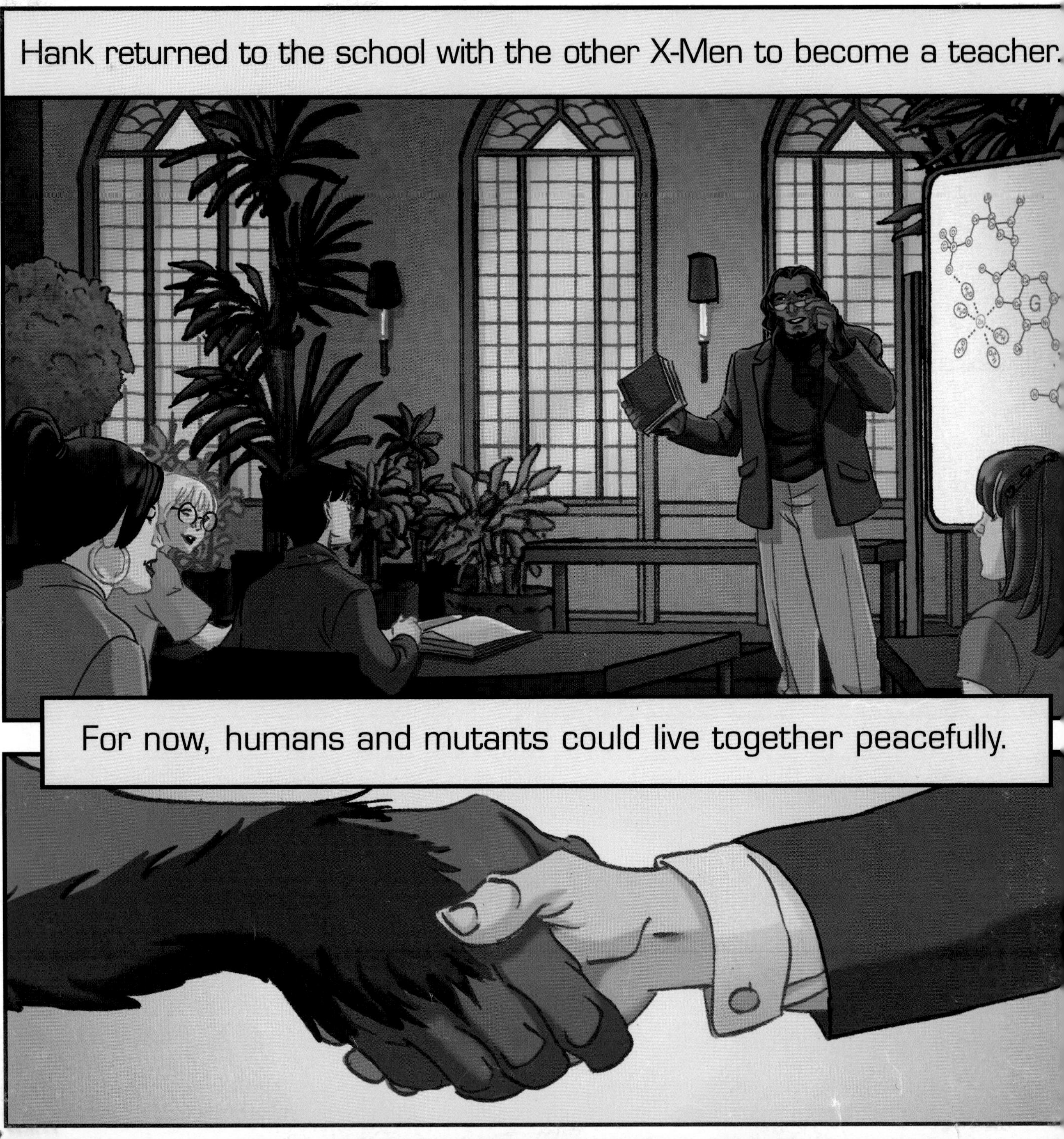
Hank returned to the school with the other X-Men to become a teacher.
For now, humans and mutants could live together peacefully.